The Sleepover Club

*Have you been
invited to all these
sleepovers?*

The Sleepover Club at Frankie's
The Sleepover Club at Lyndsey's
The Sleepover Club at Felicity's
The Sleepover Club at Rosie's
The Sleepover Club at Kenny's
Starring the Sleepover Club
The Sleepover Girls go Spice
The 24-Hour Sleepover Club
The Sleepover Club Sleeps Out
Happy Birthday, Sleepover Club
Sleepover Girls on Horseback
Sleepover in Spain
Sleepover on Friday 13th

Sleepover Girls at Camp

by Fiona Cummings

Collins

An imprint of HarperCollinsPublishers

The Sleepover Club ® is a Registered Trademark
of HarperCollins*Publishers* Ltd

First published in Great Britain by Collins in 1999
Collins is an imprint of HarperCollins*Publishers* Ltd
77-85 Fulham Palace Road, Hammersmith,
London, W6 8JB

1 3 5 7 9 8 6 4 2

Text copyright © Fiona Cummings 1999

Original series characters, plotting
and settings © Rose Impey 1997

ISBN 0 00 675396 5

The author asserts the moral right to
be identified as the author of the work.

Printed and bound in Great Britain by
Caledonian International Book Manufacturing Ltd,
Glasgow G64

Sleepover Kit List

1. Sleeping bag
2. Pillow
3. Pyjamas or a nightdress
4. Slippers
5. Toothbrush, toothpaste, soap etc
6. Towel
7. Teddy
8. A creepy story
9. Enough food for three midnight feasts
10. A torch
11. Hairbrush
12. Hair things like a bobble or hairband, if you need them
13. Clean knickers and socks
14. Sleepover diary and membership card

CHAPTER ONE

Don't you just love children's playgrounds? I do and I love the swings best of all. There's nothing better than flying right up into the air and whooshing back. I think everyone should go on a swing once in a while, just to clear their heads. Grown-ups as well. Especially grown-ups.

My friends think I'm crazy. They say:

"Lyndz, anybody would think *Ben* was taking *you* to the playground, not the other way round."

In case you've forgotten, Ben's my four-year-old brother. He's a bit wild. He'd much rather be bashing people over the head with his pretend sword than playing on the swings. Still, my baby brother, Spike, enjoys going to the playground, so I quite often take him. Not today though. Today I'm meeting the rest of the Sleepover Club. You can come too, if you like. In fact you've got to come, because I want to tell you all about our latest adventure. It was mega-cool.

You remember that we all belong to the same Brownie Pack, don't you? Well, just over a month ago, Brown Owl told us about this special camp she was arranging during the summer holidays.

"It's for those of you who'll soon be going up to Guides," she said.

"That's us!" said Rosie and I together.

"There's going to be a special four-day 'under canvas' camp at Foxton Glen at the beginning of August. It's a fun way to get you used to the kind of things that Guides do," Brown Owl continued.

"Cool!" shouted Kenny. "We can leave Brownies to the babies!"

"I heard that, Laura McKenzie!" said Brown Owl, scowling at Kenny.

Kenny scowled right back at her. If there's one thing she hates it's being called by her proper name. 'Laura' is way too girlie for her!

"What will we be doing at the camp?" asked Frankie, quickly changing the subject before Kenny got too out of control.

Frankie's our sort of unofficial Sleepover Club leader. She's so sensible you see.

"Well, you'll be helping to put up your own tents for a start, then there's abseiling, canoeing, a climbing wall, archery—"

"Wicked!" laughed Kenny. "It's going to be cooler than a fridge full of Magnum ice creams!" She was so hyper, I thought she was going to start bouncing round the room at any minute.

I turned to Fliss, who was sitting next to me. "What's she like!" I laughed. But then I saw Fliss's face. She was not a happy bunny. "What's up with you?" I said.

"I hate all those things," she moaned.

"You know, abseiling and stuff – it's just not me!"

She was right there. Fliss is not really an outdoorsy kind of girl. Give her a bottle of nail varnish and a pile of magazines and she's in heaven. Shinning down the side of a building on a rope – well, that's more like Fliss's idea of hell. She's very clean is Fliss, and strictly one for her home comforts.

I couldn't help feeling sorry for Fliss. The rest of us were getting all excited about the idea of going away on this special camp and you could tell that she was starting to feel really left out. And that's another thing about Fliss – she hates to be left out of anything.

"How much will it cost?" Rosie asked Brown Owl in her quiet voice.

The rest of us looked at each other worriedly. We know that Rosie's a bit conscious about money since her father left home. But seeing as he coughed up for our trip to Spain, we hoped there'd be no reason why he shouldn't do it again for the camp.

"Well, I'm just finalising details about that," Brown Owl told her, "but it should be quite reasonable. We're hoping that Brownies from the 12th Cuddington pack will be joining us. And the more people there are, the more people there'll be to share the cost."

"Oh great!" piped up a voice. "Our friends Regina and Amanda belong to 12th, don't they, Emily?"

The voice belonged to the horrible Emma Hughes. She and Emily Berryman are our sworn enemies, the M&Ms. Just for one lovely moment I'd forgotten they were in the same Brownie pack as us. And because they're the same age as the rest of us, they'll be moving up to Guides soon, too. That meant that the Gruesome Twosome would be coming to the camp. Suddenly it didn't seem quite so great after all.

"Now, could all those older Brownies who are interested in going to Foxton Glen please put up their hands. Just so I've got some idea of numbers," said Brown Owl.

Kenny, Frankie, Rosie and I shot up our hands. So did the awful M&Ms and their friend Alana 'Banana' Palmer, plus a few more girls.

"Felicity, I don't see your hand up," said Snowy Owl, who is also Fliss's auntie Jill.

Fliss did a real cherry. Even her blonde hair looked as though it was blushing.

"I, er– I'm not sure," she stammered.

The M&Ms sniggered behind their hands.

"Oh Felicity, I'm sure you'll love it," Snowy Owl told her. "Besides, all your friends want to go. Won't you feel left out if you miss all the fun?"

Smart move, Snowy Owl – if anything was going to make Fliss change her mind, that would do it! Fliss raised her hand very slowly.

"All right!" shouted Kenny, leaping to her feet. "It'll be mega! Just think of all those sleepovers we can have!"

"I'll have a letter ready for your parents by next week's meeting, which will give details of the cost," explained Brown Owl.

"Then those of you who decide to go must bring your money the following week."

Well, you can imagine what we were like for the next week, can't you?

"This is painful!" sniffed Fliss on Saturday afternoon. We were in Frankie's bedroom, talking about the camp, as usual. "I'm sick of you going on about that stupid camp. Can't we talk about something else?"

"Like make-up?" I suggested.

"Or clothes?" asked Frankie.

"Or what about Ryan Scott?" asked Kenny, pretending to kiss Frankie's teddy, Stanley.

"Shut up!" snapped Fliss.

"Maybe you shouldn't come after all," said Rosie. "But what would you do all by yourself while we're away?"

Fliss looked really anxious, like she hadn't thought about that. She paused for a moment and then said, "Well, what do you have to do at this camp? They don't make you do loads of frightening things, do they?"

"No, of course they don't," Rosie reassured her. "Tiff used to be in the Guides and she said the camps are really wicked."

Tiff is Rosie's older sister.

"They make this mega-big camp fire," she continued, "and everyone sits round it and sings. And sometimes you actually cook your food on the fire."

That sounded a bit like a recipe for disaster for us – The Sleepover Club are hopeless when it comes to cooking – but it did sound like a laugh.

"What else do you do?" asked Fliss. "You can't spend all your time round the fire."

"There are nature trails and stuff," Kenny told her. "And on the last night there's a sort of concert and everyone has to perform in front of the others."

We all stared at her in amazement.

"What are you looking at?" she snapped. "I've been asking Molly the Monster about it. She does have some uses. She went to Foxton Glen on an 'under canvas' camp last summer."

It was a miracle that Kenny had managed to ask her sister Molly anything without World War III starting. To say that they don't get on is like saying that Ronan Keating is gorgeous: it's kind of stating the obvious.

"So it's not all big and scary then?" asked Fliss. She definitely looked a zillion times brighter now.

"No way!" laughed Frankie. "Guides do the same kinds of things as Brownies, only they're a bit more adventurous. And I bet you'll be able to think of something really awesome to perform at the concert!"

Fliss grinned this big grin. "It does sound kind of cool," she laughed. "I thought there might be one of those awful assault courses, and I'm dead scared of those. You know, crawling over those nets and through all that mud and everything. Urgh!" She did this big dramatic shiver. "But that's just crazy, right? They won't have one of those, will they? Because if they do, there's absolutely no way that I'm going to this camp."

We all looked at each other.

"What's up with you lot?" asked Fliss.

"Nothing," said Rosie and Frankie quickly.

"Assault course!" guffawed Kenny loudly. "I wish!"

"Hic!" I gulped. You can always rely on me to get hiccups when things get a bit awkward.

"Hey, Fliss, can you go down to the kitchen and get a glass of water for Lyndz?" asked Frankie. She started to knead my hand with her thumbs – a trick that usually cures my hiccups.

As soon as we were sure that Fliss was downstairs, we all started to talk at once.

"But there *is* an assault course at Foxton Glen, isn't there?" asked Frankie.

"Yep and Tiff says it's pretty awesome, too," nodded Rosie.

"And isn't there an Assault Course Challenge at the end of the camp?" asked Frankie again.

"There sure is," confirmed Kenny. "Monster Features told me all about it. Teams race against each other and there's a

16

trophy for first prize and everything. Molly's team came second, so we've got to win when we go."

"But... hic... Fliss won't go... hic... if she finds out... hic... about that," I said between hiccups.

"Well we won't tell her then, will we?" decided Kenny.

"We won't tell who what?" asked Fliss rushing in with my glass of water. I took it from her and started to drink.

"We won't, um, tell Brown Owl that Kenny snores," said Frankie quickly.

As soon as she said that I took a big gulp of water and started to choke. Kenny started to slap me on the back – really hard.

"Yes, because someone who went to camp with Molly snored," Kenny told Fliss, "and Brown Owl made them pitch their tent right in the middle of the wood, miles away from the others."

Fliss's eyes became enormous. "Seriously?" she asked anxiously. "I'd hate that. You won't tell her about Kenny's snoring, will you?"

"Of course we won't!" Frankie reassured her.

"Um, Kenny, you can stop hitting me now," I yelped. "I'm not choking anymore. And my hiccups have gone!"

That was the last time we spoke about the camp before the next Brownie meeting. We figured that if we didn't mention it at all, then Fliss wouldn't find out about the assault course at Foxton Glen. She'd sounded deadly serious about not going if there was one, and it would be awful to go away without her. The Sleepover Club tends to do everything together, and having a sleepover without one of us there would feel too weird. It was going to be a real challenge to keep the assault course a secret from Fliss, but of course it was crucial that she didn't find out.

CHAPTER TWO

The following week, the rest of us waited for Fliss outside the church hall before our Brownie meeting.

When she appeared, Kenny hissed, "Right, not a word about the assault course!"

Fliss walked over to us. She looked in a real mood. "I suppose Brown Owl will be going on about that stupid camp again," she said crossly.

"Well, a 'Hello, how are you?' would have been nice!" joked Kenny.

"And there's no need to sound so enthusiastic about the camp!" laughed

19

Frankie. "We wouldn't want you to actually enjoy yourself now, would we?"

"I'm not sure that I'm going to go," Fliss said.

"What?" we all yelled.

"But you said you *were*, last time we talked about it." Rosie sounded exasperated.

"Yes, I know, but I want to find out whether or not there's an assault course there," explained Fliss. "And I can't ask Auntie Jill because Mum says that she's on a course from work or something. She won't be coming to Brownies for the next few weeks."

"That's a pity!" said Kenny innocently.

If Fliss didn't have the chance to ask Snowy Owl about the assault course, she probably wouldn't find out about it until we were safely at camp. And by then it would be too late!

"I don't understand what the big deal is about an assault course anyway," I said. "I mean, even if there *is* one – OUCH!" I suddenly fell to the ground.

"Whoops, sorry, Lyndz. I think I must

have tripped you up," said Kenny. As she bent to help me up, she hissed in my ear, "I told you not to mention the assault course."

"I know – but—" I spluttered.

"Goodness, Lyndsey, that was quite a tumble. Are you all right?" Brown Owl asked, as she ushered us into the hall.

I nodded and gave Kenny a dirty look.

At the start of our meetings Brown Owl always runs through everything we're going to do. When she mentioned the camp and the letters to take home we all held our breath. We were sure that Fliss was going to ask her about the assault course. But Brown Owl said that we'd a lot to get through and sort of hurried us into our sixes to work on our Season's Badge, so Fliss didn't get the chance.

As we're not all in the same six, we didn't meet up again properly until the end of the meeting when Brown Owl was handing out the letters about the camp.

"Don't forget – I need your parents'

permission slips and your money by next week," she reminded us.

Emma Hughes and Emily Berryman jostled and pushed us to make sure that they were the first ones to get their sweaty little paws on the letters.

"Pathetic!" spat Kenny.

"We'll see who's pathetic when we beat you in the Challenge at the end of the camp!" sneered Emma Hughes.

"Oh yeah? We'll see about that!" retorted Kenny.

The M&Ms tossed their hair and stalked away.

Fliss, who was next to me at the back of the group, asked anxiously, "What Challenge?"

"Um, I'm not sure," I said quickly. "It's probably who sings the best songs round the camp fire or something."

"Oh great," said Fliss. "I love singing like that, we'll probably win the Challenge – easy!"

"Oh you think so, do you, Miss Prissy-Knickers?" snarled Emma Hughes, who had suddenly appeared out of nowhere. "Well you'd better start practising. I wouldn't have thought a weed like you would be much good at—"

"I've got your letters," Frankie said loudly. She quickly thrust two letters about the camp at Fliss and me, and stood between us and the M&Ms.

"Crikey, Fliss, look at the time!" said Rosie who had joined us. "Your mum'll be wondering where we are!"

"Better run along to mummikins!" mimicked the Gruesome Twosome.

Fliss went bright red.

"You should go, too," shouted Kenny. "It's getting windy now and we wouldn't want you to take a wrong turn on your broomsticks!"

We all screamed with laughter and, linking arms, we ran as fast as we could out of the hall and down the path.

Fliss's mum and my dad were waiting for us outside. Rosie went with Fliss and I'd arranged to give Kenny and Frankie a lift home. When we'd waved goodbye to the others, the three of us piled into Dad's van and Frankie pretended to collapse in a heap.

"Phew, that was close!" she said, wiping her brow dramatically.

"I know!" I squealed, "I couldn't believe it when you got into a row with the M&Ms, Kenny. I thought Fliss was bound to suss something out."

"Then when the M&Ms had a go at her about winning the Challenge," giggled Kenny, "and she thought they were talking about singing!"

We all exploded into laughter.

"Do you think she's going to find out about the assault course before the camp?" I asked when we'd calmed down.

"I hope not," said Frankie.

"There's only a week before we have to give in the forms. And once she's paid her money, Fliss can't really back down, can she?" reasoned Kenny.

"We'll have to avoid the M&Ms, though," said Frankie. "They could easily mention the

Assault Course Challenge again, and that would completely finish Fliss off!"

When we'd dropped Frankie and Kenny off, I started to panic. It wouldn't be easy avoiding the M&Ms because we're all in the same class at school. The camp was planned for the summer holidays but we had one week at school before the end of term. The only way we could be sure that the M&Ms wouldn't mention anything to Fliss was if we kidnapped her and kept her in a cupboard. The thought was tempting but a bit impossible. We would just have to stay on our toes and be extra wary of them.

For that last week, every time we saw Emma Hughes or Emily Berryman, we bundled Fliss out of the way. Or we started to talk extra loudly, so that even if they did say anything Fliss wouldn't be able to hear it.

On the last day of term we all went a bit wild. We seemed to spend more time outside than we did in the classroom. We were too hyper to work and even Mrs

Weaver, our teacher, knew it. The M&Ms seemed to be spending a lot of time leaping over obstacles – a bench, the rubbish bin, Ryan Scott.

"Sad!" said Kenny loudly as she passed them.

"You won't be saying that when we beat you in the—" started Emma Hughes, and we all knew what she was going to say next.

"Hey, Fliss, look!" Rosie dragged Fliss away.

"Daisy chains!" screamed Frankie, in an over-the-top kind of way. "Let's make daisy chains with those younger children."

"Yes!" I said, trying my best to sound enthusiastic. "Let's!"

After that narrow escape we just had to stay out of the M&Ms way for the rest of the afternoon. It was a huge relief all round when school finally broke up. And it was even more of a relief when Fliss turned up at the next Brownie meeting with the form and her money. There was no going back now – assault course or not!

*   *   *

There were only two weeks between us handing in our forms and actually going away to camp. You can imagine how excited we were. We never seemed to talk about anything else.

"I can't wait!" laughed Kenny.

We were all sitting in her room a couple of days before the camp. "There'll be so many cool things to do! I've always wanted to have a bash at abseiling!"

"Yeah, 'having a bash' is probably right!" laughed Frankie. "Knowing you, you'll probably try to do it too fast and splat! – you'll be squashed on the wall."

Fliss sort of shivered.

"We're only joking Fliss," I reassured her. "It won't be like that – there'll be lots of fun stuff. It's going to be brilliant!"

"Do you think we ought to start practising for the Challenge?" Fliss asked.

We all stared at her with our mouths open.

"What, you mean you know?" asked Rosie.

"Yes," said Fliss slowly, as though we were all dummies. "And I really think we should

27

practise so that the M&Ms don't beat us."

"Cool!" shouted Kenny. "Maybe we should go outside now and start climbing a few trees or something. What about press-ups, they're good."

I started to shake my head at Kenny, because I could see Fliss's shocked face.

"How will climbing trees help us to sing the best songs round the camp fire?" she asked.

Kenny looked blank. It wasn't often that she was speechless.

"It's something to do with opening your lungs properly." Frankie leapt to her rescue. "I've heard that you should exercise before you sing."

Rosie and I rolled our eyes at each other, and I tried not to giggle.

It was a relief when we were finally on the minibus heading for Foxton Glen. We knew that we couldn't keep the assault course a secret from Fliss for much longer, but we figured that we'd cope with it when it happened. Besides, we already had enough to worry about, dealing with the low-down behaviour of the M&Ms.

We'd all been lining up to get on the minibus, when they barged past us and nabbed the seats right in the middle. Alana Banana sat on the seat opposite them, which meant that we couldn't all sit together. So Kenny and Frankie sat in front of the Gruesome Twosome, Rosie and Fliss sat behind them and I sat in front of Alana Banana with – get this – Brown Owl. So we had an excellent journey to Foxton Glen – not! And it was all the fault of those selfish M&Ms. We were determined that they'd pay for it over the next few days.

"Here we are, girls!" Brown Owl called out, as we finally swung off the main road onto a twisty track. We all pressed our faces up to the windows so that we could see where we'd be staying for the next few days.

"Wow, isn't this cool!" yelled Kenny. "What's that over there?" She was pointing to something in the distance.

"That's the tower for the abseiling and the climbing wall," explained Brown Owl.

The minibus stopped.

"Right, can you please get off the minibus quickly and quietly," said Brown Owl, "and remember to collect all your bags."

We pushed and shoved our way off as quickly as we could. Apart from Fliss, who always has to check anywhere a million times to make sure she hasn't left anything behind.

We were all hyper, laughing and joking as we looked around – it was awesome. But we also realised that the dreaded moment had finally arrived.

"What are you so excited about?" Fliss asked, when she finally joined us.

Together, we pointed at the sign in front of us, which said, in huge letters: ASSAULT COURSE THIS WAY.

CHAPTER THREE

Poor Fliss! I've never seen anyone go as white so quickly. It was as though someone had sucked all the blood out of her face with a straw.

"Are you all right, Felicity?" Brown Owl asked anxiously.

But Fliss could only mumble and point to the sign.

"Assault course does sound a bit grim, doesn't it?" laughed Brown Owl. "But don't worry, because it's not going to be the assault course for much longer. I'll explain when the other Brownies get here."

Another minibus was driving towards us. When it stopped, the Brownies from 12th Cuddington spilled out. We recognised a few of them from school. We certainly recognised Regina Hill and Amanda Porter, who headed straight for the M&Ms and Alana 'Banana'. They stood in a silly little huddle screeching and chattering like chimps in a zoo.

As soon as they had settled down, Brown Owl explained what she had meant about the assault course. This camp was going to have the theme of children's TV programmes, so the assault course was going to be referred to as Blue Peter, the kitchen would be Grange Hill, and the toilet and shower blocks would be called Arnold and Doug!

There were twenty Brownies altogether, eleven from our pack and nine from the other. So there were going to be four tents of five, plus a tent for the grown-ups. The Sleepover Club were in a tent together and we didn't have to share with anyone else which was great. The M&Ms were sharing with Alana Palmer, the awful Amanda Porter and Regina Hill. Then there was a tent of Brownies from 12th Cuddington and another tent with girls from both packs, but it was OK because they all knew each other.

Brown Owl called each group a 'patrol' and we all had a name. We were Rugrats, the M&Ms and their group were Teletubbies, the group just from 12th were The Simpsons and the mixed group were Wombles. Pretty cool, huh? We really laughed when Brown Owl said that we had to call her Tom and the Brown Owl from 12th, Jerry!

A group of forest rangers had already started to put up our tents. Jerry said that three of them would be staying with us for the rest of the camp and we had to call them Paddington, Garfield and Scooby Doo!

I wondered how I would ever remember all those new names.

"Isn't this great?" I said to Rosie, as we took our stuff over to the tents.

"Yeah, but I don't think Fliss is very

happy," she replied. I looked across at Fliss. She looked really sulky and miserable.

"Right, Rugrats, this will be your tent," said Brown Owl. "This is Paddington and her ranger friends. You can help them finish putting up your tent, but you must do exactly as they say."

The rangers were really cool and fun. And actually I think they were quite pleased with us, because Kenny and I are used to putting up tents. We go camping a lot with our families, you see. We helped tighten the ropes and everything, while Frankie and Rosie tried to calm Fliss down. I just couldn't understand how anyone could get so freaked out over an assault course – especially one that was called Blue Peter. Still, Fliss does a lot of stuff that I don't understand.

When our tent was up we took our stuff inside. The tent itself was like a bell and had one big pole in the middle. We arranged our sleeping bags so that they fanned out like the spokes of a wheel. We would sleep with our heads in the middle by the pole, and our feet pointing out to the sides. It was a bit weird, but exciting, too.

I kind of like sleeping in a tent because it's all sort of squashed and cosy. But Fliss didn't like it at all. "There's just no room!" she kept wailing.

"Oh Fliss, shut up, will you!" snapped Kenny. "You knew it wasn't going to be The Savoy!"

Fliss's lip started to quiver a bit. The last thing we needed was any waterworks.

"Come on, Fliss, you'll get used to it!" I reassured her. "We're Rugrats, remember!"

"I wonder which Teletubbies the M&Ms are!" laughed Frankie.

"I don't know, but Amanda Porter definitely looks like one!" said Kenny and did and impression of her waddling along. We all laughed – even Fliss!

Brown Owl poked her head through the tent flap. "I'm glad to see that you're settling in," she said. "I expect you're all itching to get out and start doing things. So, go to

Arnold if you need to, then I'll meet you at Blue Peter in five minutes!"

"Great!" yelled Kenny.

She flew out of the tent, but the rest of us hung back. Fliss had started to do her impression of a quivering jelly again.

"I'm sure you won't have to go on the assault course if you don't want to," I told her.

"I'm rubbish at stuff like that, too," Rosie reassured her. "We'll go on it together. If we don't like it, we can always get off."

Fliss looked a bit brighter.

"And I'll stay with you, too," I told them. I quite like assault courses and things but I felt sorry for Fliss, and I thought that if Rosie really did want to have a proper go on it, I could look after Fliss.

"C'mon you lot. What's keeping you?" yelled Kenny. She rushed back into the tent all out of breath. You could tell that she was itching to go on the assault course.

"I'll go with action man here," said Frankie. "One of us had better keep an eye on her!" And she ran after Kenny.

The rest of us took our time. We went to the loos and when Fliss had played about in there as long as she possibly could, we made our way over to the assault course.

To be honest with you I didn't really know what to expect. I suppose I'd imagined scramble nets about six metres high and nothing but mud all around. But it wasn't like that at all. Actually it looked really pretty – there were big bushes on each side and it followed a sort of loop, so you could see where you started and finished but you couldn't see all the bits in between. It looked vast, but that was only because instead of there being one obstacle, there were two of the same kind next to each other. I guessed that that was so teams could compete against each other. Which reminded me about the Challenge on the last day.

"At last!" called Brown Owl when she saw us. "I thought Arnold must have swallowed you up!"

Two Brownies from The Simpsons ran past us. They were giggling together and looked as if they were having a great time. I couldn't wait to start.

"Fliss is a bit nervous about the assault— I mean, about Blue Peter," Rosie explained.

Fliss looked really annoyed with her.

"There's nothing to be worried about," Brown Owl reassured us. "Jerry and I are here to help you and the rangers are on the course, too. Just take your time and have fun."

"Come on, Fliss!" smiled Rosie. "We might as well have a go on it now we're here."

"Look, I'll go first, then you just follow me," I suggested.

Fliss nodded, so I set off. First you had to jump over a hurdle, then there was a ditch with a tree trunk over the top. The Brownies in front of me balanced on the trunk as though it was a tightrope. They moved along it really slowly so that they didn't fall into the mud underneath. I just copied what they did. It was great. I could hear Kenny and Frankie ahead of me, but I couldn't see them. I turned round. "Are you OK?" I shouted back.

Rosie gave me the thumbs-up sign and Fliss was actually laughing.

"You see," I called back. "There was nothing to worry about, was there?"

Once I knew that they were all right I just did my own thing. There were lots of things I'd seen people do on the television, like running through two rows of tyres, which was much more difficult than I'd thought it would be. But the hardest thing was getting over the top of the scramble nets and climbing down the other side. It took a while to get used to swaying about while you were climbing, but it was really exciting.

From the top of the nets, I could see the rest of the course. There was Emily Berryman slumped by the side of the underground crawl-through tunnel. She looked as though she was about to be sick. Amanda Porter was stuck in the swinging tyres and Kenny was pretending to be Tarzan on the rope swing. I climbed down the netting as fast as I could. I was desperate to have a go on the rest of the course.

I was just coming up to the underground tunnel when I heard screaming. It didn't register at first, but then I realised it was Fliss. I ran back and there she was – stuck at the top of the scramble nets.

"I can't move!" she cried. "I'm too scared."

Rosie was at the other side trying to coax her down. I climbed up to Fliss and tried to reassure her.

"You've done the worst part," I said. "All you've got to do now is reach over and pull yourself over to the other side."

"Easy for you to say!" Fliss squeaked.

I climbed up and showed her what to do, but it was no good, she just wouldn't move. When she'd been there for what seemed like hours I said, "There's Scooby Doo over there, talking to the M&Ms. I'll call her over, shall I?"

As soon as I said that, Fliss flung herself over the top of the nets and sort of slid down the other side. Rosie and I scrambled down after her. Fliss was lying in a heap at the bottom.

"I told you I hated assault courses!" she sobbed.

"Don't worry, you won't have to go on it again," I told her.

Me and my big mouth!

When Fliss had recovered enough, we all walked round to the end of the assault course, where everyone else had gathered.

"Have a little problem, did you?" Emma Hughes asked Fliss cattily.

Fliss blushed.

"Had a few little problems yourselves!" retorted Kenny, looking from Emily Berryman to Amanda Porter. Then it was their turn to look embarrassed.

"We'll still beat you bunch of losers in the Blue Peter Challenge!" said Emma Hughes angrily.

"Blue Peter Challenge?" whimpered Fliss, as the truth suddenly hit her. "You mean the Challenge is over the assault course?"

Kenny ignored Fliss and faced the M&Ms full on. "There's absolutely no way you're going to beat us!" spat Kenny. "And that's a promise!"

The rest of us looked at each other. When Kenny wants something badly enough, the rest of us have to suffer for it. But we didn't know then just how badly Kenny wanted to beat the M&Ms.

CHAPTER FOUR

After we'd all had a go on the assault course, Brown Owl took us to look round some of the other activities we'd be doing at Foxton Glen. Kenny was still mad at the M&Ms. I thought she'd never get over it. She didn't even perk up when we walked over to the climbing wall and the abseiling tower.

"What's up with her?" I mouthed to Frankie. But she just shrugged her shoulders.

And Fliss wasn't a bundle of laughs, either. She was still all twitchy about the assault course and kept saying there was no way that she was ever going on it again, Challenge or not. That of course just made Kenny madder still.

It didn't help that Emma Hughes and her stupid friends kept whispering together, then looking over at us and giggling.

"They're really getting on my nerves!" said Rosie.

"You and me both," I replied.

We were all a bit on edge because we were expecting Kenny to have a go at them at any moment. But luckily she didn't. She just kept giving them evil looks.

We were walking back towards our tents when Rosie pointed to something and asked Brown Owl what it was.

"That's one of the nature ponds," Brown Owl explained. "There are a few frogs and things in it, so we can look at the creatures in their natural habitat."

"They won't get into our tents, will they?" asked Fliss anxiously.

"No, Felicity, they won't hop that far!" laughed Brown Owl. "And we won't be eating frogs' legs for supper either. But we will be eating pasta and Teletubbies are on kitchen duty, The Simpsons will be waitresses and Rugrats are going to be our orderlies. Wombles, you can be on litter patrol – you should be good at that!"

We all laughed.

"So, Emma," Brown Owl continued, "when we get back to the tents could you and your patrol get yourselves ready for a bit of action in the kitchen. The rest of you will be playing games with Jerry and the rangers until supper."

Kenny had been very quiet while we were out, but when we got back to our tent she started leaping about.

"Looks like the old Kenny's made a comeback!" laughed Frankie.

"I've got a plan. It's totally brilliant and it's going to finish off the M&Ms once and for all!" she told us.

"Well go on then – spill!" I commanded.

"No way! I'm going to keep this one quiet. But you'll hear about it soon enough!" she said, grinning from ear to ear. "All I want you to do is cover up for me if anyone notices I'm missing."

"Charming!" said Fliss. "You won't tell us what you're going to do but you want us to cover for you. That doesn't sound very fair!"

The rest of us rolled our eyes. Fliss is very big on things 'being fair'.

"Just do it, OK!" commanded Kenny in a tone of voice which told us that we shouldn't mess with her plans.

In our bags we'd all brought enough goodies for three midnight feasts. Kenny had brought hers in a large ice-cream carton. She went over to her bag, took it out, and tipped everything in it onto her sleeping bag. Mini Mars bars, jelly babies, lollipops and Black Jacks spilled everywhere. She scooped them back into her bag and skipped out of the tent with the ice-cream carton.

"What on earth is she going to do?" asked Frankie, staring after her.

"You know what she's like," said Fliss.

"Do you think we should follow her to make sure she's not doing anything stupid."

"She'd kill us if she spotted us," said Rosie.

"We'll just have to do as she says and cover for her," I said. "I can hear the others outside. Come on, let's go and play some games!"

We ran outside and joined The Simpsons, Wombles and the rangers. Then we had a cool time playing an enormous game of Cops and Robbers. When someone asked where Kenny was, we just said that she had a stomach ache and was lying down. But then of course Jerry thought she ought to go and check on her, so I had to think fast.

Unfortunately, tripping up and gashing open my knee was the only thing I could think of. And very painful it was, too – I hope Kenny appreciated it. Still, it kept Jerry occupied and stopped her worrying about Kenny.

When Tom called us all for supper, Fliss looked really panicked. "What if they go to fetch Kenny and find she's not there!"

she said.

But just then, as if she was a mind-reader, Kenny appeared. She strolled out of our tent with a humungous grin on her face, and muddy marks on her trousers.

"Are you feeling better now?" asked Jerry. "Do you think you might be able to manage a little supper?"

"You bet, I'm starving!" Kenny replied.

"B– but what about your stomach ache?" squeaked Rosie.

"I haven't got one," Kenny looked puzzled, then she cottoned on. "I mean, it's gone now," she said.

"The lie-down must have done you good," said Jerry.

Kenny just smiled.

We all went to sit down and The Simpsons brought us our food.

"Mmm, this isn't half bad!" said Kenny, slurping down her pasta like a pig.

We all looked at her really suspiciously. The M&Ms had cooked it and she never praises anything that they're involved in.

"You haven't sabotaged it, have you?" asked Frankie suspiciously.

"Get real!" laughed Kenny. "I'm hardly likely to ruin the food we've all got to eat now, am I?"

"So what have you been doing?" I asked.

But Kenny just shook her head and kept tapping the side of her nose. "You'll find out soon enough," she told us.

When everyone had finished eating, we got up to collect the plates.

"Nice meal!" Kenny whispered to Emma Hughes, as she took her plate.

The M&Ms looked at Kenny suspiciously, but she just smiled and took the plates into Grange Hill.

After pudding we had to wash up, which didn't sound like much fun. I hate washing up at home, but then I'm not in the middle of a field acting stupid with my friends, am I? We had a real laugh – though we seemed to wash more of each other than the plates! I noticed that Kenny was already kind of wet, but she wouldn't say why.

By the time we'd finished, we were all soaking. And kind of tired. Have you noticed how when you're at home you just want to stay up late, but the first night you're away you want to go to bed early, just because it's all new?

It seemed like everyone felt the same because we were all yawning as we sat outside singing. I'd assumed that there'd be a camp fire every evening, but there wasn't one that first night, which was really disappointing. Brown Owl said it was because they take a long time to prepare, but she promised we'd have one on the other nights.

It was nearly dark as we all trooped back to our tents to collect our toilet bags. As soon as we got there, Kenny grabbed her ice-cream carton and peeped out of the tent flap.

"What are you looking for?" Frankie whispered.

"The M&Ms," Kenny replied. "Ssh, they're coming!"

She hurried back inside and waited for them to walk past. She was holding tightly to the carton she was holding. There seemed to be a lot of water sloshing about in it.

"Right, you lot go to Doug and delay the Gruesome Twosome and their mates as long as you can. Understood?" commanded Kenny.

"Yes, Sir!" Frankie, Rosie and I saluted her together. Fliss just looked cross.

"I wonder what she's got planned," said Rosie as we walked to the shower block.

"Dunno," shrugged Frankie, "but it certainly looks like it's something big!"

"I don't see why she couldn't let us in on it, though," moaned Fliss.

"She must have her reasons," said Frankie. "Anyway, remember, we've got to delay the M&Ms as long as possible."

We all went into the shower block. The girls from The Simpsons patrol were just leaving. They smiled and said "Goodnight".

"They're really friendly, aren't they?" said Fliss.

"Unlike some people," said Rosie, scowling at the M&Ms.

"Where's your horrible little friend?" asked Emma Hughes.

"Kenny? She's got a stomach ache," replied Frankie.

"Something serious I hope," smiled Amanda Porter.

The rest of her group laughed their stupid little laughs.

"It must have been something you cooked," said Fliss, who was hovering in the doorway.

"Well you certainly didn't eat much," Emma Hughes snapped. "I would have thought a wimp like you should be building up your strength. You're going to look a complete wally when you get on the assault course again."

Fliss went bright red. But so did Emily Berryman and she started to walk towards the door.

I think we all panicked a bit then. Fliss more than the rest of us. As she was in the doorway, it was up to Fliss to stop Emily Berryman as she went past. And Fliss definitely wasn't up to giving her a rugby tackle. She started dithering, dropped her toilet bag and stooped to pick it up. Berryman didn't notice and tripped over her. Then all the stuff from her toilet bag spilt all over the floor and she ended up falling on top of it. It was like something out of a cartoon, but we couldn't have planned it better if we'd tried.

We all bent down to help pick everything up. And of course Frankie, Rosie and I kept picking up Emily Berryman's things sort of accidentally-on-purpose. So it took quite a while to get everything sorted out.

"You're so clumsy!" snarled Emma Hughes to Fliss as they were leaving.

"So is *she*," Rosie said, looking at Emily Berryman. "And we wouldn't want Fliss to be contaminated with any of the germs from her things."

The M&Ms and their cronies flounced out, and we all cracked up.

"What about Kenny?" wailed Fliss. "What if she hasn't finished yet?"

"Oh, but I have!" said Kenny suddenly appearing. "I've just been hiding behind a bush watching you all. Nice one, Fliss!"

Kenny still wouldn't tell us what she had done. She just had this big I'm-so-clever grin on her face and kept saying, "You'll find out soon enough!"

We all finished washing and brushing our teeth, then went back to our tent to get ready for bed. We did our striptease in our sleeping bags, then sat in a circle round the pole in the middle.

"Let's have our midnight feast now!" I said. "I'm so tired, I don't think I can keep awake much longer!"

The others laughed. I'm always the first one of us to fall asleep.

We emptied all our sweets onto Kenny's sleeping bag. Her ones looked a bit gross because they'd been loose in the bottom of her bag and were covered in all sorts of bits of fluff.

"How do we decide what we're going to eat for our midnight feast tonight and what we're going to save?" asked Rosie.

"You mean, how are we going to stop ourselves from eating everything in one go?" laughed Frankie.

"And how do we stop the swamp monster breaking in and stealing all our sweets?" said Kenny in a really spooky voice.

"Don't!" squealed Fliss.

"I'm not scaring you, am I?" asked Kenny, in the same spooky voice.

Before Fliss could answer, a loud piercing scream seemed to rip through the campsite. We all clung together, hardly daring to breathe.

CHAPTER FIVE

"What was that?" squeaked Frankie.

"I don't know, but it came from the tent next door," said Rosie.

We all looked at each other.

"The M&Ms!" we said together.

"It sounds as though Brown Owl's in there now," said Fliss.

We all went to the tent flap and peered out. We could hear someone wailing and we were pretty sure that it was Emma Hughes. Then we heard Brown Owl.

"I'm sure it's just a freak thing, Emma," she was saying. "Why on earth would anyone want to put a frog in your sleeping bag?"

Well, we just collapsed in a heap when we heard that.

"A frog!" squealed Frankie to Kenny. "You actually put a frog in her sleeping bag!"

Kenny was nodding and spluttering.

"Sssh! Brown Owl's coming!" said Fliss.

We all dived into our sleeping bags.

"Are you all right in here, girls?" asked Brown Owl.

"What was that noise?" asked Fliss in her weakest little voice.

"Oh, nothing to worry about," said Brown Owl. "You haven't been into the Teletubbies tent for anything, have you?"

"Oh no, we wouldn't do that!" said Kenny.

"Hmm," said Brown Owl thoughtfully. "I don't want there to be any trouble. I want this to be a happy camp."

"Oh, but it is!" gushed Rosie. "We're having a great time, aren't we?"

"Yes!" we all spluttered, trying not to laugh.

"That's good!" said Brown Owl. "You're

cooking tomorrow, so you'll have to be up by seven. I'd try to get some sleep if I were you! Sweet dreams!"

When we were sure that Brown Owl had gone, we all turned on our torches and sat up.

"That was wicked!" I squealed.

"I just hope the M&Ms don't suss out who it was and do it back to us, though," shuddered Fliss. "I'd die if I found a frog in my sleeping bag."

"We'll have to try not to leave our tent for too long tomorrow, just in case," said Frankie seriously. "And we'd better make sure that the flap is tightly shut tonight."

Kenny and I got up and fastened it as securely as we could. Not even King Kong would have been able to get through when we'd finished with it!

"Anyway, we should be celebrating getting one over the M&Ms!" said Kenny. "Chocolate frog anyone?"

We collapsed in giggles again.

Our midnight feast goodies were still scattered over Kenny's sleeping bag. We scooped them all together again and roughly divided them into three piles. We put what we weren't going to eat that night into two plastic bags and left them by the tent pole.

I ate what felt like my weight in chocolate and declared, "I'm stuffed now!"

"Me too!" agreed Rosie.

"I guess we ought to try to sleep if we've got to be up early tomorrow," suggested Frankie.

I expected Kenny to disagree, but she was already snuggling down in her sleeping bag. "Seven o'clock!" she grumbled. "What sort of crazy time is that?"

It felt strange to be having a sleepover in a tent. Especially as we were all suddenly too tired to sing our sleepover song. But at least we had another two 'under canvas' sleepovers to look forward to.

Are you all right there, I'm not walking too fast, am I? The playground isn't too far away now, then we can have a go on the swings. I bet Kenny will be a lot livelier today than she was on that first morning at camp. Boy is she grumpy when she gets up. Especially when Brown Owl has woken her up at the crack of dawn!

"Tell her to shut up!" moaned Kenny, pulling a pillow over her head.

The rest of us dragged ourselves out of our sleeping bags and wandered around bleary-eyed. But by the time we'd got ourselves dressed, and dressed Kenny because she said she was too tired to do it herself, we were ready for anything. Well, almost anything, we weren't ready for the M&Ms, that's for sure.

As soon as we saw them, we knew we were in trouble.

"We'll get you for that!" hissed Emma Hughes, as we dished out baked beans and toast.

"I don't know what you're talking about!" Kenny said innocently.

"You'll be sorry, that's all!" said Emily

Berryman, snatching her plate from me.

"What do you think they'll do?" whispered Fliss. "I hope they haven't been into our tent while we've been cooking breakfast."

We rushed back to the tent as soon as we could, but nothing seemed to be missing. We felt inside our sleeping bags, too, but there were no frogs in any of them.

"We can't stay in the tent all day!" said Fliss.

"We won't have to, all the patrols are doing different activities, so we'll be spread out across the site," explained Frankie. "And we'll be back at the campsite together for lunch, so if the M&Ms go anywhere near our tent we'll know about it."

"I suppose we'll just have to hope that their group doesn't get back before us, won't we?" said Rosie.

We didn't have the chance to worry about that for long; we soon became busy trying to encourage Fliss down the abseiling tower. I mean it wasn't really high or anything, Fliss was just in scaredy-cat mode. It's crazy. You know that she can do something, but she doesn't think she can and wimps out.

Paddington came abseiling with us, as well as another cool instructor from Foxton Glen called Danny. Whenever he called Fliss forward, she'd go to the top of the tower, take one look down and go all feeble. I felt a bit sorry for her, especially as Kenny kept having a go at her.

"Fliss don't be such a baby!" she yelled. "Look at all the ropes round you! It's absolutely impossible for you to fall, isn't it, Danny?"

"Sure is!" said Danny. "I'm holding tight onto you up here!"

He winked at Paddington, who blushed big time.

I thought Fliss was going to be up there all day. We tried encouraging her. Kenny tried threatening her. We even tried bribing her with new nail varnish, but nothing worked.

Then she saw the M&Ms. They'd been doing some archery and were heading back to the campsite for lunch. Amanda Porter suddenly turned to look at us and saw Fliss hovering about at the top of the tower. She said something to the M&Ms and they both turned round. Then they started to walk towards us.

I could see Fliss getting more and more panicky. She looked as though she was going to topple off the tower in fright. Especially when the awful witches started to cluck like chickens and flap their arms about. But that kind of spurred her on.

"Right, I'm going down now," Fliss suddenly told Danny.

She turned round and started to abseil down the tower slowly. We all yelled and shouted encouragement. When she got to the bottom, Fliss sort of wobbled about while Paddington removed her harness.

"That was cool!" laughed Kenny. "Now we know how to get you to do stuff – we'll just ask the M&Ms to come and make fun of you!"

The Gruesome Twosome and their

cronies were already walking back towards our tents. I was so glad that Fliss had proved them wrong. But that's Fliss – she can always produce a surprise when you're least expecting it!

When we got back to the campsite we had to make sandwiches for everyone's lunch, which was a bit of a drag. But the other patrols had to collect wood for the camp fire, which sounded even more of a pain. Our patrol was going to help Brown Owl actually build the fire later in the afternoon. I couldn't wait.

While we were making the sandwiches, we took it in turns to keep popping back to check on the tent. Until Brown Owl became suspicious. But by then all the others were hanging round waiting for their lunch anyway.

"I bet the M&Ms are too scared to break into our tent," said Kenny confidently. "One-nil to us!"

"Let's hope it stays that way!" said Frankie grimly.

After lunch we had just the best time canoeing. We had to concentrate so hard on what the instructor told us that we didn't have a moment to even think about the M&Ms. By the time we got back to our tent, I was exhausted. And then we had to go and get everything ready for dinner round the camp fire. It's hard work being a Brownie sometimes!

It was pretty cool helping Brown Owl build the fire. It's a lot more difficult to light than it looks and it seemed to take ages before we even saw any smoke. Then gradually it built up and the flames got quite fierce. It could have been kind of dangerous, I guess, but we were all given a talk about not getting too close and not acting stupid around it. Even Kenny took notice of that. And we also had a fire drill with pretend buckets of water, so that if it did get out of hand we'd all know what to do.

For supper we were having jacket potatoes wrapped in foil and baked in the fire. They were going to take quite a long time to cook, so while we were waiting Brown Owl asked each patrol to go off on their own and come up with a song, dance or poem they could perform in front of the others the following evening.

Kenny did her I-told-you-so face and Fliss looked really excited. I think she was all set to start practising one of our dance routines straight away, but Kenny was having none of that. "OK, let's start training for the Blue Peter Challenge!" she said.

Fliss went white. "B– but I'm not going on the assault course again," she stuttered.

"Look, Fliss, if you can master the abseiling wall, the assault course will be a doddle," Kenny reassured her. "Just imagine the M&Ms are laughing at you!"

"Thanks a lot!" said Fliss crossly. "Anyway, we're supposed to be working on our performance for tomorrow night!"

"Don't be so wet!" said Kenny. "We're always doing silly dances at our sleepovers, we know loads of routines really well already. But we haven't done any practice for the Challenge. Let's all sprint down to our tent, do ten sit-ups, sprint back and do some press-ups!"

We knew by the tone of her voice that she was deadly serious.

"Come on! We want to win this thing, don't we?" she yelled and hared off.

The rest of us ran after her, gasping and wheezing. We were totally exhausted by the time Brown Owl called us for supper. It was as if we were in the army, the way Kenny was putting us through our paces. It was a real relief to sit down and eat our baked potatoes!

Fortunately we weren't sitting near the M&Ms, so they didn't put us off our food. But I don't think anything would have put me off the marshmallows we toasted over the fire for pudding. They were yummy!

After we'd eaten, we all sang songs round the fire which was well cool! We sang 'Camp Fire's Burning' in rounds, 'Do Your Ears Hang Low?' with all the actions and we finished off with 'Taps' – which is what we always sing at the end of Brownie meetings.

Tired, but happy, we all staggered back to our tents. We were almost there when Kenny stopped us. "Sssh!" she hissed. "There's someone in our tent!"

CHAPTER SIX

We stopped in our tracks and listened. Kenny was right, there was certainly somebody rustling about inside our tent. It just had to be those M&Ms.

"Right, I'm going to get them for this!" whispered Kenny.

She started to tie up the tent flap.

"Don't let them get out whatever you do," she warned. "And try not to let them know you're here."

She ran off towards Grange Hill. We didn't know what she had in mind. We were too busy worrying about what we'd do if the

M&Ms tried to get out.

Kenny was back in a flash. She was carrying a huge tube of squirty cream.

"You haven't stolen that, have you?" Fliss looked shocked.

"'Course not," Kenny replied. "I've just borrowed it."

She bent down and quietly began to undo the tent flap. Then we all crouched on the ground, so that when the M&Ms appeared we would be ready for them.

"I think they're coming out!" hissed Rosie.

We all stood up. My heart was beating like crazy. When the tent flap opened we all started screaming and Kenny sprayed cream like a demon. It was only when this tall blob started squealing and stumbling into us that we realised it wasn't the M&Ms at all. It was Snowy Owl – Fliss's Auntie Jill!

"What on earth is going on here?" asked Brown Owl who had come across because of all the noise we were making.

"We thought that someone had broken into our tent," explained Kenny sheepishly.

"Well as you can see, no one has," said Brown Owl. "Fliss's mum sent her some clean underwear and Snowy Owl was putting it in your tent."

Brown Owl looked furious, but fortunately Snowy Owl was laughing. "I finished my course this afternoon," she explained, "so I came down to join the camp. I thought I'd surprise you, Felicity, as I haven't seen you for such a long time! But I guess I should have just given you your underwear, rather than sneaking into your tent."

Fliss was as red as a beetroot. I think it was because everyone had heard about her mum sending down some clean underwear. She was more embarrassed about that than the fact that we'd covered her Auntie Jill with cream.

All the other Brownies had gathered round us. Unfortunately the M&Ms were right at the front, sneering at us, which was just awful.

"At least there's one good thing," said

Frankie when Brown Owl had sent everyone away and we were cleaning up the mess.

"Oh yeah, what would that be then?" asked Kenny.

"The M&Ms haven't managed to sabotage us today," said Frankie gleefully. "I bet they couldn't think of a way to get back at us. They're just not bright enough. Shame, isn't it?"

We all laughed.

We were ready to go to the shower block with our toilet bags when Kenny said, "Let's sprint to the showers, do push-ups against the wall, shower and stuff, and then jog back!"

Now I like Kenny as much as anyone, but this was getting a bit out of hand. It really was like being in the army. Besides, we were all totally exhausted.

"Get real, Kenny!" moaned Frankie. "This camp is supposed to be fun."

"But we've got to win the Challenge!" said Kenny. It was like it was the only thing that mattered to her.

"I've already told you I'm not going on the assault course again," Fliss said. "And I'm going to tell Auntie Jill that I'm not tomorrow. She won't make me do anything I don't want to."

Kenny screwed up her eyes and looked at us all in a fury. "Well I'm going to beat the M&Ms, even if you're all going to wimp out." She spat out the words and sprinted off towards the showers.

We all looked at each other, then trotted after her.

Fortunately, it was quiet when we got there. I think the other Brownies must have washed while we were apologising to Snowy Owl and cleaning everything up. It had taken ages to wash all the cream off the tent. Some had even got onto Rosie's sleeping bag.

We were a bit sticky with cream ourselves, so we all decided to have a shower. There was a cubicle for each of us, but unfortunately there wasn't any hot water left. We were all absolutely freezing by the time we'd got out and dried ourselves.

"Well at least that's cooled us down!" laughed Rosie. "Maybe we should jog back to our tent after all – just to warm up a bit!"

So after brushing our teeth, that's what we did. We laughed and giggled all the way back, which sort of broke the tension a bit, because we were still feeling a bit annoyed with Kenny. She was so obsessed by the whole Blue Peter Challenge that she was starting to spoil the camp for the rest of us.

When we got back we could hear the M&Ms in the tent next door. They were obviously having a midnight feast, although it was nowhere near midnight yet.

"Aren't these Choc Dips just scrummy!" Emma Hughes was saying.

"Mmm, they can't be as gorgeous as these milk bottles!" said Emily Berryman in her gruff voice. We sometimes call her 'the Goblin' because of her deep voice – and because she's so small.

The other Teletubbies were all cooing over their sweets too.

"You'd think no one else had ever had a

midnight feast before!" grumbled Kenny. "They're just so pathetic."

She started to howl like a wolf and the rest of us joined in.

"Oh grow up!" shouted Emily Berryman. "We know it's you, Laura McKenzie. Couldn't you think of anything more original?"

Kenny looked furious. But before she could say anything Emma Hughes piped up, "Is Felicity there?"

Fliss pulled a face then said, "Yes, what do you want?"

"Hadn't you better go and put on that underwear your mummy sent?" Emma Hughes asked in a sickly voice. "You dirtied your other knickers at the top of the abseiling tower, didn't you? You're a big baby, Felicity DirtyBottom!"

We couldn't see Fliss's face because it was kind of dark, but I could tell that she was blushing by the heat that was coming off her! She hates people making fun of her, and she's especially prickly about her surname – it's Sidebotham, but nobody ever says it like that!

Amanda Porter joined in taunting poor Fliss. "You'll need even more clean underwear when we've wiped the floor with you in the Blue Peter Challenge!" she smarmed in her silly fat voice. "You all will!"

"Come on!" Kenny said through her teeth. "We're not going to listen to these idiots. They're all talk – no action!"

We scrambled back into our tent. Nobody spoke. We got undressed and ready for bed in complete silence, for just about the first time ever!

After what seemed like ages Kenny said quietly, "Now do you see why we've got to train hard to beat them?"

We all nodded. Except Fliss. "I'm still going to tell Auntie Jill that I don't want to take part in the Challenge," she mumbled.

Before Kenny could have another go at her, Frankie leapt in. "Well, we'll all need our strength, won't we?" she laughed. "What about a few munchies before bedtime? If those stupid M&Ms can make such a lot of noise when they eat their midnight feast, we can make twice as much when we eat ours!"

"Yes!" we all shouted at the tops of our voices.

We all scrambled about around the tent pole, but before we could find the sweets we'd saved for that night's feast a torch flashed through the tent flap. We all jumped, but it was only Brown Owl.

"I don't know what's going on between you and Emma and her friends," she said firmly. "But whatever it is, I want it to stop."

"It's not just us—" Rosie started to protest.

"I know and I don't want to hear any more," said Brown Owl. "I've spoken to the girls next door and they promised me that whatever petty squabbles you've had in the past are over. I hope you can say the same thing."

We could feel her staring at us all, although we didn't dare look her in the face.

"Well?"

"Yes, everything's fine now," mumbled

Frankie. "There won't be any more trouble."

We all nodded our heads reluctantly.

"I'm very pleased to hear it," Brown Owl smiled. "So get some sleep, because you've another busy day tomorrow. Breakfast round the camp fire first thing! Sleep well!"

Kenny and I fastened the tent flap behind her, then we turned to the others.

"What do you reckon to that?" said Rosie.

"Well, I guess if that's what the M&Ms said – and meant it – we'll just have to play it cool with them until camp's finished," I said.

"But what about the Challenge?" asked Kenny.

"We'll have to abandon it!" said Fliss sounding livelier than she had done for days.

"I don't know about that," said Frankie quickly. She knew that Kenny wouldn't give in so easily. "I think we should have our midnight feast and sleep on it!"

We all looked around the tent again and rummaged about in our bags. But none of us could find any sweets.

"OK, this isn't funny!" Kenny sounded

very agitated. "Who's got the grub? One of you must have taken it from the tent pole."

We all shook our heads, then we looked in our bags again. And in our sleeping bags, our toilet bags and our wellingtons. Nothing!

"You don't think Snowy Owl took it, do you?" asked Rosie. "She was in here, wasn't she?"

"Don't be crazy, she wouldn't do that!" said Fliss indignantly. "I reckon it's the M&Ms. They must've been eating our midnight feast!"

Just then we heard lots of giggling outside our tent.

"That's right, Knicker Girl!" screeched Emma Hughes. "And very scrummy it was, too!"

"OK, that's it!" screamed Kenny. "This means war!"

And by the look in her eyes, we knew that she meant it.

CHAPTER SEVEN

I don't think any of us slept well that night. It's just not the same having a sleepover without a midnight feast! And I guess the rest of us were worried about what kind of revenge Kenny was planning for the M&Ms. She definitely had something in mind, because she kept mumbling about it in her sleep.

"Splat Goblin's face," she murmured. "Kick Hughes water."

None of it made sense of course, and in the morning Kenny denied saying anything at all. But she was still determined to get back at the M&Ms. Big time!

"We've got one more day to get ourselves in shape for the Assault Course Challenge!" she told us as soon as we woke up. "So we're going to train for it in every spare minute we have."

The rest of us groaned. Fliss pursed up her lips but didn't say anything.

"Teletubbies are on cooking duty, aren't they?" said Rosie.

"I think so, why?" asked Frankie.

"I was just thinking that we could raid their tent and try to get our midnight feast back while they're busy," replied Rosie.

"We could do," said Kenny, "but I'm starving. Let's go for breakfast first, or I'll waste away!"

We got dressed as fast as we could and ran to the toilet block. Everybody else must have had the same idea because there was a massive queue.

"Oh man!" moaned Kenny, jiggling about. "I'm going to wet myself if we have to wait much longer."

"You should all start wearing nappies!" smirked Emma Hughes, who was just emerging from Arnold. "We've always known that you were babies!"

Frankie and I had to use all our strength to stop Kenny from swinging for her. But even by the time we'd got to the front of the queue, Kenny was still seething. "Stupid witches!" she was mumbling. "I'm going to get them!"

Fliss, in contrast, hadn't said anything. In fact she'd hardly spoken since we got up. She kept looking round as though she was searching for someone. As soon as we got to the camp fire and she saw Snowy Owl, she sprinted over to her.

"Looks like she's going to get out of the Blue Peter Challenge," Rosie whispered to me. But I wasn't so sure. Fliss wasn't looking too happy. We left Frankie to try to calm Kenny down, snatched some toast from Emily Berryman in Grange Hill and wandered over to Snowy Owl.

"But I'm terrified of going on the assault

course, Auntie Jill!" Fliss was moaning. "And I'm no good at it anyway."

"That's a ridiculous attitude, Felicity," said Snowy Owl sternly. "You don't know what you're capable of until you try it."

We quietly went to sit down beside Fliss.

"That's what being a Guide is all about," continued Snowy Owl. "It's about gaining confidence in things and learning some independence."

"Fliss, don't worry about the Challenge," I said. "We'll help you."

Rosie nodded and squeezed Fliss's arm.

Snowy Owl smiled at us. "And it's about working as a team," she said. "You can only try your best, Fliss, that's all anybody asks of you. Right, girls, I'll leave you to it."

She left us looking into the fire, not really knowing what to say to Fliss.

"She's changed," said Fliss slowly. "Just because that course she went on from work used an assault course as a 'team building exercise' she thinks everybody should go on one!"

Poor Fliss, her aunt had suddenly gone all assertive on her, and her chance of getting out of the Challenge had gone.

"Look Fliss, try to look at this in a positive way," said Rosie soothingly. "You're as sporty as any of us. You can easily manage the assault course, it's just a case of believing in yourself."

"Yeah," I agreed. "So instead of looking at the scramble net and thinking, I'm going to get stuck at the top of that, you've got to think, it's just like climbing up a wobbly fence and that's easy!"

Fliss looked at us and smiled a watery kind of smile. "I guess so!" she mumbled.

Before we had time to reassure her some more, Kenny came flying towards us. "Operation Sweety Rescue is on for lunchtime!" she said. "We're going to raid the M&Ms tent while they make lunch."

It sounded fun, but I wasn't so sure it was going to be that easy.

Before lunch our patrol had a go at archery. It was well cool. And Fliss was good at it, which boosted her confidence no end. In fact she became quite a pain, reminding us how much better she was at archery than the rest of us.

"It's a pity there's no archery in the Challenge then, isn't it?" said Kenny sharply.

That soon shut Fliss up.

Kenny was still way too obsessed with the Challenge. At lunchtime, as we were walking back to the campsite, she even told us all what our weaknesses were.

"You don't take it seriously enough," she told Frankie. "And Lyndz, you don't put enough effort into it. Rosie, you're always looking round to see what everybody else is doing, and Fliss, well you're just a wimp, aren't you?"

That was really the last straw. We were all sick of Kenny telling us that we should be training all the time. I mean this wasn't the Olympics, was it? It wasn't even Gladiators. It was just some end-of-camp competition, which was supposed to be a bit of a laugh.

"If that's your attitude, Kenny, maybe we

shouldn't compete at all," said Frankie angrily. "I'm sure you're more than capable of beating everyone else single-handed."

It was really weird hearing Frankie speak to Kenny like that. They've been best friends like forever. But I guess that's why she could say what the rest of us were only thinking.

Back at the campsite Frankie headed straight for our tent. The rest of us followed her, but Kenny slunk off on her own.

"I'm sick of her going on like that," Frankie told us. "She's spoiling everything."

"Imagine how *I* feel!" said Fliss. "She's always calling me a wimp and putting me down."

"I know, and it's not fair," Rosie reassured her.

I looked out of the tent flap and I could see Kenny just sort of mooching around by herself. I felt kind of sorry for her. She was only trying to get one over the M&Ms and the rest of us wanted to do that, too. It's just that sometimes Kenny gets too carried away. I left the others to their complaining and went to see if she was all right.

"Hiya, Lyndz," she said kind of sheepishly when she saw me. "Is everything OK?"

"Pretty much," I told her. "But I think you've upset everybody."

Kenny just shrugged. Then she brightened up. "Maybe they'll forgive me if I get our midnight feast back from the Gruesome Twosome's tent," she said excitedly. "Will you help me?"

I wasn't so sure. I mean it's all right when all five of us do something like that together, but what would happen if just the two of us got caught?

"Come on, Lyndz, please," Kenny pleaded. "The M&Ms are preparing lunch, I've just checked. It won't take a minute."

Kenny was already undoing the flap of the M&Ms tent. Well I couldn't let her do it all by herself, could I? I went and joined her.

"I'll stay here," I whispered, "to keep a lookout!"

"It'll take too long for me to look through their stuff by myself," Kenny whispered back. "You'll have to come in, too, and we'll keep checking to make sure that no one's coming."

Very reluctantly, I crept inside.

Although the M&Ms were sleeping in the same kind of tent as us, it looked completely different. In our tent there was stuff all over the place, whereas in theirs everything was in neat piles at the bottom of each sleeping bag. It had this nasty smell of very stinky socks, too.

I didn't really like rummaging about in other people's things, but I told myself that they'd done it to us

"I can't find anything. What about you?" I asked Kenny. "You don't suppose they ate everything, do you? Or maybe they took the sweets with them, just in case we did this."

"Nah," replied Kenny confidently. "I saw them leave and they certainly didn't have anything with them. And not even that fatty Amanda Porter could have eaten all our sweets in one sitting."

We rummaged about some more, but it was hopeless.

"I'm going to kill them for this!" hissed Kenny.

Then a voice outside asked, "Kenny? Lyndz? Is that you?"

My heart nearly jumped out of my mouth.

"It's me, Frankie." She popped her head through the flap. "I think lunch is ready and I reckon the M&Ms could be back at any minute. You'd better hurry up!"

"Come on, let's go!" I said to Kenny. I grabbed her by her sleeve and she stumbled and fell – right into the line of wellies neatly arranged at the edge of the tent. As they all toppled over like dominoes, sweets began to spill out.

"Oooh, gross!" squealed Kenny. "They've been hiding our sweets in their boots!"

"Never mind that now!" I screeched. "Come on!"

We grabbed the bags of sweets and flew out of the tent. Frankie pushed us into our own tent just as Brown Owl was coming round the corner.

"Lunch is ready, girls!" she said, popping

her head through the flap. "Didn't you hear me calling?"

"Sorry, we've just been talking about how much we're enjoying ourselves here," gushed Rosie.

"Well that's great, but we're toasting sandwiches round the fire and we really all need to be together for that," said Brown Owl.

"We'll be right there!" said Frankie.

We waited until we were sure Brown Owl had gone, then we all collapsed into giggles. Kenny and I tossed the bags of sweets onto the floor of the tent to show the others. Then we shoved them right to the bottom of her sleeping bag – no one would dare to look for anything in there!

"Our sweets have probably been contaminated by those stinky M&Ms," Kenny said, pulling a face.

"At least we've got them back," said Frankie. "Thanks, you two."

"That's OK," said Kenny.

I raised my eyes to her. "And…" I

prompted.

Kenny looked puzzled.

"You're sorry…" I continued.

"Oh yes. I'm sorry I was awful about you competing in the Assault Course Challenge!" she said in a huge rush.

"We can only try our best," said Frankie. "You must remember that, Kenny."

Kenny nodded. "I'll try," she said sheepishly. Then she brightened up. "I've got a new recruit for our team, too," she told us, grinning from ear to ear.

"Who?" we all asked together.

Kenny wriggled about a bit and pulled something from underneath her jumper. It was a teddy bear. "I've kidnapped him from the M&Ms tent," she told us smugly. "And if they want to see this bear alive again, they're going to have to show us a bit of respect!"

CHAPTER EIGHT

Before we could ask Kenny what she was planning on doing with the bear, she leapt up and said, "Come on, let's go for lunch. I'm starving."

Kenny has a bottomless pit of a stomach.

When we got to the camp fire, everyone else was already there. The M&Ms looked at us suspiciously, but we just ignored them. As Teletubbies were on cooking duty, it was their job to hand round the food. Fortunately Regina Hill gave us ours, so we weren't too worried about the M&Ms tampering with it in some way first!

We were each given a piece of silver foil, which was a bit weird. But it made sense when we were given two slices of buttered bread and some thin pieces of cheese. We had to put one piece of bread butter side down on the foil, put on the cheese, then the other piece of bread, butter side up. Then we folded the silver paper round it like a parcel and gave it to Snowy Owl to shove into the embers of the fire. The sandwiches cooked for five minutes then she turned them over and after another five minutes they were ready. Scrum-mee!

After we'd eaten, Brown Owl reminded us that as it was our last night we would all be performing something round the camp fire. We had totally forgotten about it, so we went into a mega-panic.

"We'll just have to work on one of our dance routines," said Frankie.

"But when will we have time?" asked Fliss. "We're orienteering round the whole of Foxton Glen this afternoon. It's going to take ages."

"We'll just have to practise our dance between the control points," said Kenny.

And that's just what we did. We must have looked crazy doing our All Saints meets the Spice Girls routines next to the climbing wall and across the archery field. We had to sing, too, which made it difficult because we were all singing at slightly different speeds. We're used to doing our routines to proper cassettes – singing along at the same time isn't as easy as you'd think.

"This is never going to work!" grumbled Fliss. "Everyone's going to laugh at us."

"Not if they know what's good for them!" warned Kenny. "Which reminds me, I've got this little baby here to take care of." She pulled the teddy she had stolen from the M&Ms tent out of her pocket.

"What are you going to do with it?" asked Rosie.

"I'll show you," Kenny replied.

We were standing next to the frog pond. Overhanging it there was a tall straggly bush.

"There we go!" laughed Kenny, leaning over and wedging the bear between some of its branches.

"Should we leave the M&Ms a ransom note or something?" I asked Kenny.

"Then they'd know it was us who'd stolen it, wouldn't they?" said Fliss, looking all panicky. "And we'd get into trouble."

"But so would the M&Ms, because if they dobbed us in to Brown Owl, we'd have to tell her about them sneaking into our tent and stealing our midnight feast," reasoned Kenny.

That was certainly true, but it still seemed a bit risky.

"What should we put in the note?" asked Rosie. "We can't really ask for money or anything, can we?"

"We should call a truce until after the Assault Course Challenge tomorrow," suggested Frankie. She's always very sensible.

"Then if we win, we know that we've won fair and square!" I laughed.

"What do you mean *if* we win," shouted Kenny. "Of course we're going to win. Now – race you to the next control point!"

Unfortunately, we were heading for the dreaded Blue Peter. We hadn't been near it since the first day and Fliss nearly flipped when she saw it again. She went all white and trembly. I really thought she was going to pass out.

"Come on, Fliss," I reassured her. "Remember what we said – you're as capable as anyone of competing tomorrow. Just take it a bit at a time."

Snowy Owl was waiting on the assault course, because you're not allowed on it without an adult there. She could see that Fliss was in a state, and encouraged her to go on it for a few minutes to conquer her fear. Fliss just didn't want to be there, but of course she was under heavy pressure from the rest of us to give it a go. I felt really sorry for her actually. But she did OK – she even got over the scramble nets.

But then, as usual, Kenny went and totally

destroyed her confidence. "We'll never win if you're such a snail," she yelled. "Hurry up, for goodness' sake!"

Fliss froze and couldn't carry on. The rest of us were furious with Kenny.

"Shut up!" Frankie yelled at her. "Fliss is doing her best. We're sick of you telling us what to do! I don't know why you don't just leave us alone."

Oh no! Not again! It was awful. Frankie and Rosie comforted Fliss, who slid down the rope swing and said she couldn't carry on. Kenny went off in a sulk by herself and I had to try to pretend to Snowy Owl that everything was all fine and dandy!

How we finished the orienteering without a major punch-up, I'll never know. But worse than that was having to perform together in the show around the camp fire that evening. We'd hardly practised anything and we weren't speaking to Kenny. Well, I was, but the others weren't. And we hadn't had the chance to tell the M&Ms that we'd kidnapped one of their teddy bears. But that was the least of our worries.

The camp fire itself was mega-cool. Or it would have been if we'd been our normal Sleepover Club selves. As it was, we felt that there was a huge rift between us all. If we were supposed to be Rugrats, then Kenny was definitely Angelica, bossing the rest of us around. So when we were getting our jacket potatoes ready and preparing our billie-cans for apple crisp, Kenny sat a little way from us, muttering to herself.

We had a good laugh anyway because the stupid M&Ms greased the inside of their billie-cans with Fairy Liquid, instead of the outside. So when they started cooking over the camp fire all their ingredients were soapy and frothing inside. Yeuch!

While our potatoes were baking and the apple crisp was cooling, we put on the show. Each patrol took it in turns to perform for the others. We were dreading it, but nothing could have prepared us for what happened next.

It started off OK. The girls from the

Wombles sang a really funny song called 'What's the Use of Wearing Braces', then The Simpsons told a really spooky ghost story about some Guides who got lost at camp, which made us go all goosepimply and huddle together. We wanted to get ours over with, but no, Emma Hughes insisted that Teletubbies went next. Can you guess what they did? Pretended to be Teletubbies, of course. How original! In Amanda Porter's case it didn't take too much imagination. She was already bright red all over and her hair stands up in a funny curl, so she was a dead-ringer for Po!

When it was finally our turn, we decided to sing and do a routine to 'I Know Where It's At'. We were pretty sure that Kenny didn't want to join in, so Frankie said, "There's just the four of us, because Kenny's not feeling very well." She flashed a look at Kenny, who flashed it right back.

"I'm feeling very well, thank you," she said. "I'm joining in, too."

Frankie rolled her eyes at the rest of us

and we all took up our positions. Kenny made sure that she was right at the front. Frankie counted us in and we were off. To start with we were all singing at different times, and I could see the M&Ms and their silly friends spluttering behind their hands. That of course made Kenny really mad, and suddenly she took off into this crazy dance routine which we'd never practised before. The rest of us carried on singing and dancing as best we could, but Kenny was the centre of everyone's attention. And I have to admit she was pretty amazing.

I don't remember exactly what happened next, it all seemed to happen so fast. Kenny's head must have been in something of a spin because she was moving like a maniac. But she was also dancing pretty close to where the M&Ms were sitting. I'm almost certain that I saw Emma Hughes stick out her foot, and the next thing we knew Kenny had stumbled and was staggering near to the fire. Then she let out a cry. It was a cry like I'd never heard before.

We all rushed over to her. Brown Owl had moved fast when she saw Kenny careering towards the fire, but she hadn't got there fast enough to prevent her from falling.

"Are you all right?" asked Frankie anxiously, looking at Kenny who was sprawled on the ground.

"My ankle hurts," Kenny replied, grimacing with pain.

Brown Owl bent down and checked it over carefully. "Well you haven't broken it," she told her, "but you've sprained it quite badly. I'll bandage it up now and then your father can look at it when you get home tomorrow."

You know that Kenny's dad's a doctor, don't you? And Kenny is fascinated by all that medical stuff, too, so she was in her element, even if she did look as white as a sheet. Everybody was crowding round her, the M&Ms as well, and Emma Hughes had a particularly nasty smirk on her face.

When Brown Owl had bandaged Kenny's ankle, Frankie and I helped her up and supported her as she hopped over to the nearest log.

"*I* was sitting there!" said Emily Berryman nastily.

"Well you'll just have to sit somewhere else, won't you!" said Snowy Owl coolly. "And I want you to look after Kenny and make sure that she has everything she needs."

That made Kenny laugh out loud. "I'm going to enjoy this!" she told us, as she made Emma Hughes fetch her potato from the fire. Then, what with one thing and another, she made them run about after her all evening. We were in stitches watching them scurrying about like ants. Especially as you could tell that they were hating every minute of it!

It was only later when we were finally in bed – it had taken Kenny hours to get to the toilet block and back – that we realised just how much Kenny's injury was going to affect us.

"What about the Blue Peter Challenge?"

asked Rosie suddenly. "How are we going to compete in it now?"

All the colour drained from Kenny's face. I really thought she was going to cry.

CHAPTER NINE

"The Assault Course Challenge!" Kenny kept moaning. "I was determined to win it and now I can't even take part!"

The rest of us looked at each other. I felt desperately sorry for Kenny, but I couldn't think of anything to say which would make her feel better.

"Maybe I can still compete in it," said Kenny, sounding brighter. "If I'm careful I should be all right."

"Don't be stupid!" Frankie said. "You'd only do yourself more damage." She looked at the rest of us, then back at Kenny. "I know you've been driving us crazy about this whole Challenge thing," Frankie continued, "but as it's so important to you, we'll try to win it for you, as a sort of get-well present!"

Fliss didn't look too sure about that. "But I can't do it," she wailed, her eyes filling with tears. "What if I let you down?"

"You can do it and you won't let us down!" Kenny told her. "You just need confidence. And I'll be there to cheer you on!"

Now that didn't sound like a good idea at all.

"I won't be having a go, I promise!" she reassured us. "And I'm not going to say this again, but I'm sorry about getting carried away before. I hate falling out with you guys!"

We all gave each other a group hug round the tent pole.

"Crikey, that was like something out of 'Friends'!" laughed Kenny and we all collapsed into giggles. Apart from me. I collapsed into hiccups.

"Lyndz, you do pick your moments!"

laughed Frankie, digging her thumb into my palm.

"I'm… hic… sorry!" I giggled.

Suddenly there was an enormous thumping on the side of our tent.

"Oi! You! Have you been into our tent?" It was Emma Hughes.

"And stolen our midnight feast?" asked Amanda Porter.

"That was *our* midnight feast, I think you'll find!" replied Kenny.

"Well you must have stolen teddy Egbert, too," snivelled Emily Berryman. "And I want him back."

"Can't baby sleep without her 'ickle bear then?" asked Rosie in a babyish voice.

"You've stolen him and I'm going to tell Brown Owl!" The Goblin sounded very upset.

"Go ahead and we'll tell her about you stealing our things," said Kenny. "And I'll tell her how you tripped me up, Hughesy. You could have damaged me for life!"

There was silence. Then a few seconds

later we heard Brown Owl. "Really, Emma, I thought you would've known better than to be prowling about at this time of night. Get back to your tent, now. I don't want to hear another sound out of you!"

We waited until she'd gone, then started laughing.

"It's not often those two get into trouble!" laughed Fliss. "They're usually such goody-goodies!"

"It serves them right," I laughed. "And hey, my hiccups have gone! It must have been the shock."

"Well that calls for a celebration!" said Kenny and fished out the sweets from the bottom of her sleeping bag. "Here's to being friends again!"

We toasted each other with fizzy cola sweets.

"And to beating the M&Ms in the Assault Course Challenge!" I said. But as soon as I'd said it, I wished I hadn't. Fliss began to look very troubled again.

"Fliss, you'll be brilliant!" Kenny

reassured her and she sounded serious. You could tell that it meant a lot to Fliss to hear Kenny say that. In fact it really cheered her up. And whose idea do you think it was to do a conga round our sleeping bags at one in the morning? Right, Miss Sidebotham herself. I fell asleep when the others started to sing 'Wannabe', doing all the dance moves in their sleeping bags, and Frankie told me they didn't get to sleep until after three!

You could tell that they'd had a late night because I was the only one who was wide awake at seven o'clock. The others were all bleary-eyed and moany. Not the best start to a day when the reputation of the Sleepover Club was on the line!

"Come on, guys!" I yelled at them. "We've an important day ahead of us!"

They all groaned and staggered out of their sleeping bags, and they didn't seem to wake up properly until after they'd eaten breakfast. It was a good thing they woke up then because we had the craziest time after that. We had to pack all our stuff away and take our bags to the minibus, then we had to help the rangers take down the tents and make sure the camp fire had been put out properly. There was just so much work for three nights of camping, but it had been worth it. And of course the real highlight – for us anyway – was still to come. Yep, it was finally time for the long-awaited Assault Course Challenge.

We all lined up at the start of the course and Brown Owl explained a few things to us. "Now, there'll only be four girls competing from each patrol," she said. "Kenny has an injured ankle and one girl from each of the other patrols has told me that she's not keen on taking part in the Challenge either. Those girls are now managers and official cheerleaders!"

Kenny led the cheering and Fliss looked furious. "If you hadn't hurt your stupid ankle, I wouldn't have had to compete in this after all!" she hissed to Kenny.

"Now, as there are two sets of obstacles

and four teams, Jerry and I are going to be timing each team. The Challenge is going to be based on the overall time each patrol takes to complete the course," continued Brown Owl, "so you're not just competing against the team next to you, you're competing against the times of the other teams as well. Do you all understand?"

Everyone nodded.

"I hope we're not teamed against the stupid M&Ms," I whispered to Frankie.

"Right, listen up," said Brown Owl. "The Simpsons and the Wombles will be competing together and Teletubbies will be teamed against Rugrats."

We all groaned.

"Just our luck!" said Rosie.

"So if those of you taking part for The Simpsons and Wombles can line up here, we'll get started!"

We moved away from the starting line, which was pretty crowded. Everybody seemed to be deciding on who was going to go first from each team. The M&Ms were skulking around, too.

"So which of you has wimped out then?" Kenny asked them.

Amanda Porter went bright red.

"Well that's no surprise, is it? You're so big you'd probably get stuck in the underground tunnel!" laughed Fliss.

I don't like people being criticised just because they're a bit bigger than everybody else, especially as Fliss once did that to me. But Amanda Porter is truly awful, so she deserved it.

"Where's my bear, anyway, you thieving little snakes?" asked Emily Berryman.

"You'll only see it again if you agree to play fair in this challenge," Frankie told them firmly. "If you try to pull any stunts, your bear will be a dead ted. Understood?"

The Goblin looked shocked. She looked round at her friends and they all, reluctantly, nodded.

"OK then. May the best team win!" laughed Kenny.

We went back to join everybody else at

the start of the course.

There was a lot of cheering as the first two teams set off. The Wombles were awesome. A girl called Rachel Sunderland went off first for them. She was like a real little monkey swinging her way over all the obstacles.

"Wow! Look at her go!" cooed Kenny. "I hope you're all taking notes!"

Fliss started jiggling up and down. I could sense how nervous she was. With the next two girls, The Simpsons started catching up a bit, so by the time the fourth competitors were going over the obstacles it was really tight.

The Wombles last competitor was Hannah Williams. We knew her from school and she's brilliant at games, in fact she's the captain of our netball team. She flew over the scramble nets as though they weren't there. It was amazing.

"We'll never beat their time!" I said.

"Yes we will!" Kenny told us confidently. "Right, we're on. Lyndz, you go first to give us a good start, then Fliss, then Frankie. Rosie, you're last, so you've got to be prepared to do the business for us!"

We all huddled together.

"Do this for me!" Kenny told us. "And let's whip the pants off those stupid M&Ms!"

We all broke away and did a high five.

"Pathetic!" spat Emma Hughes.

"We'll soon see who's pathetic!" said Kenny knowingly.

Then it was my turn to go.

As soon as Brown Owl blew her whistle I charged down the course. I could hear Kenny yelling, but I wouldn't let myself look at her. I raced over the hurdle and balanced on the log without falling in. It was wicked! I felt like I was flying. It was almost as good as galloping on a horse.

"Come on, Lyndz! You're miles ahead!" shouted Kenny. "Regina Hill's rubbish!"

By the time I had crawled through the tunnel and back over the scramble nets, I knew that I was way in front. It was a great feeling swinging across the ditch on the rope swing, I could have done it all day. But there were more important things to think about. I just had the swinging tyres to negotiate, before handing over to Fliss. I could see her at the line waiting for me. I'll never forget her face. She was dead white and looked as though she was about to throw up. I whizzed through the tyre swing and threw myself at the line.

"It's a piece of cake, Fliss. You're way ahead, just enjoy yourself!" I panted.

Fliss didn't look capable of enjoying herself, but as soon as I'd touched her hand she set off. We all held our breath. This was Fliss's moment to shine, if only her nerves didn't get the better of her.

CHAPTER TEN

Now, I have to tell you that from the start it didn't look good for Fliss. It took her about three attempts to get over the hurdle, and that wasn't even high. I thought she was going to have kittens when she had to run across the log and risk falling in the mud underneath.

"Come on, for goodness' sake," Kenny was muttering under her breath. "Alana 'Banana' is catching up."

"You're doing great, Fliss," I shouted. "Take your time and you'll be fine." And don't look at Kenny's angry mush, I wanted to add.

"You've got to encourage her," I told Kenny. "That's what Fliss responds to."

Kenny tutted and shouted, "Great Fliss! It's running through the tyres next and that's no problem."

Actually, it really wasn't a problem. Fliss is so light and nimble that she just danced through them as though they weren't there.

"Great stuff!" Kenny and I cheered.

Alana 'Banana' had fallen off the log twice by now and was looking really muddy and fed-up. Fliss was way in front. But the dreaded scramble nets were looming.

"OK, Fliss, take your time!" I shouted. "Just think about a wobbly fence, that's all it is!"

Fliss's face was a picture of concentration. You could almost hear her grit her teeth as she put her head down and went for it. Snowy Owl was at the bottom of the net shouting encouragement. But I think it was Kenny shouting "The M&Ms are watching Fliss, show 'em what you're made of!" which really inspired her. She shinned up the nets like Catwoman and threw herself over the top. It was awesome.

"Way to go, Fliss!" Kenny and I shouted, leaping about like lunatics. "You're miles ahead, just keep going."

Everything else after that was a piece of cake. It was as though Fliss had totally conquered her fears and was really enjoying herself. When she got to the second lot of scramble nets she climbed up them like she'd been doing it all her life. Was this really our wimpy Fliss? Maybe the real one had been abducted by aliens and this was an extra-terrestrial replacement! But why should we care? We were beating Teletubbies by miles.

There was one sticky moment when she lost her grip on the rope swing and had to have two attempts to get over the ditch. But by that stage it didn't matter because she was so far ahead of Alana 'Banana' anyway.

We were virtually hysterical by the time Fliss ran home. Of course Frankie and Rosie still had to go over the assault course, but we weren't worried about them. We were home and dry – or so we thought!

The first thing to go wrong was that Frankie wasn't quite ready when Fliss ran home. I think she'd expected her to take much longer and she was still tying up her shoelace when Fliss appeared. Because of that, she didn't take full advantage of the lead our team had over Teletubbies. And she was up against Emma Hughes.

At least Frankie had me, Kenny and Fliss cheering her on. We ran the length of the course yelling encouragement. Fliss was still all hyper and kept shouting how 'easy' everything was, which was a bit of a laugh considering what she's normally like. I don't think Frankie appreciated it too much, either. Especially when she got her foot caught in the scramble netting and was hanging almost upside down for a few seconds.

Emma Hughes didn't have much support at all. Amanda Porter was too fat to keep running alongside her, Alana 'Banana' was too traumatised after her experiences, Regina Hill was exhausted and Emily Berryman was waiting next to Rosie at the starting line. Still, you could tell that Emma Hughes was desperate not to be beaten by us and she raced with Frankie right to the line. So when it came to Rosie's turn, she and Emily Berryman were neck and neck.

My heart was in my mouth as they raced over the first few obstacles. But at the first scramble net it became obvious that this was going to be no contest. Berryman was green with fear – she just couldn't hack it. My friends are always telling me that I'm too soft on people, but I felt really sorry for her, even if she is one of our deadly rivals.

The noise on the course was just crazy because all the other teams were cheering as well. Rosie and Emily were the last competitors in the Blue Peter Challenge and the whole contest would be decided on their times.

"Easy-peasy, Rosie!" yelled Kenny as Rosie flew over the top of the nets. "No contest, man! The Goblin's gone to pieces."

I could sense Rosie hesitate as she looked back to where Emily was struggling. But Kenny urged her on and she ran on to the underground tunnel while her competitor was still struggling over the top of the nets.

"She's miles ahead and I bet we're faster than those Wombles, too!" laughed Kenny. "I'm going to ask Brown Owl what their time was."

She hobbled off to the finishing line where Brown Owl was standing with her stopwatch, and she didn't see that Rosie was slowing down. Emily Berryman had crawled out of the underground tunnel and looked as though she was going to throw up again. Emma Hughes was yelling at her to carry on. Her face was all screwed up in anger – not a pretty sight!

Rosie had heard all the commotion behind her as she started to climb the second set of scramble nets. She looked back and saw that Emily Berryman was in difficulties. You could tell that she really didn't know what to do.

Frankie, Fliss and I were yelling like demons so Rosie carried on climbing to the top of her net. She was just about to swing herself over when Emily started crying below her. She was clinging to the net and unable to move. Without thinking, Rosie climbed back down and said something to her, then they slowly climbed the nets together. Rosie watched Emily climb over the top first then she swung herself over. When she'd checked that Berryman was OK, she leapt down and ran like crazy. She hurled herself at the rope swing then sprinted on to the tyre swing, which was the last obstacle.

"What were you doing?" Kenny screamed at her as she crossed the line. "We were miles in front and then you threw it away. You lost us the Challenge to help one of the M&Ms of all people!" She spat the accusation out as though it was the most disgusting thing she could think of.

Rosie was still out of breath. "I'm sorry,"

she panted, "but I could see how frightened she was. I couldn't just leave her there, could I?"

"I would've done!" snarled Kenny. "Wombles only won by thirty seconds. That's thirty seconds, Rosie. You lost us that by going back to help that stupid dead-head! Some get-well present that turned out to be!"

Kenny limped off angrily and poor Rosie looked distraught. "I didn't know what to do!" she kept saying, over and over again.

When it came to the prize ceremony we couldn't bear to watch. The trophy for the winners was all gold and shiny. We'd have loved to have been the ones raising it up as though it was the World Cup.

"So near and yet so far!" muttered Frankie.

Then Brown Owl surprised us all. "We usually only have one prize in this Challenge," she told us all seriously. "But I think what we saw today deserves another one. Rosie, in the Rugrats' team, demonstrated what being in the Brownies and Guides is all about – taking the initiative to help other people even if it sometimes means losing out yourself. Today Rugrats lost the Blue Peter Challenge because of Rosie's actions. But I'm going to create a special Sportsmanship Award, and Rugrats will be the first team to receive it."

We all went wild, and everybody else was cheering us, too. Apart from the M&Ms of course! Kenny actually started to smile again and soon she was back to her normal noisy self, laughing and larking around.

Before leaving the campsite we went to retrieve Egbert, Emily Berryman's teddy bear. It wasn't as easy to get down from the bush as it had been to put up there, but we managed to hook it towards us with a stick. Kenny took great pleasure in throwing it at the M&Ms when we got on the minibus.

"Here's your bear!" she snarled. "You should've put him in your team for the Blue Peter Challenge. He'd have been better than you were, Berryman!"

Emily Berryman went bright red and looked as though she was going to cry.

Emma Hughes just looked furious.

Just to annoy the M&Ms even more we sang 'We Are The Champions' at the top of our voices for most of the way home.

Until Emma Hughes said nastily, "But you're not champions, are you? I don't see any trophy."

Surprisingly, it was Fliss, of all people, who said, "Well, we would've been if your team hadn't been a complete bunch of wimps who needed rescuing every five minutes!"

We all screamed with laughter when she said that. Emma Hughes blushed the colour of a beetroot and Emily Berryman looked as though she wished she could slip through a hole in the minibus floor.

We haven't actually got our award yet. We won't be getting it until we go back to Brownies next term. Brown Owl says she's going to have a trophy made, which is well cool. Especially as ours will be the first names on it. Kenny keeps telling us that the trophy is really hers because we said our performance in the Blue Peter Challenge was her get-well present. I don't think we meant it quite like that though.

Kenny's ankle is much better now, by the way. Her dad said she shouldn't run about on it too much so we keep threatening to wheel her about in a pram. She doesn't seem too keen on that idea. I can't think why!

Going back to our trophy – we can't wait to see it and we're all totally blissed about it, but winning trophies isn't the most important thing in life, is it? I mean, even if we didn't win the Assault Course Challenge we all had a brilliant time at camp. And in some ways we'd all changed a little when we came home. We all seem to have learnt a bit about ourselves. Fliss is still boring us stupid about her triumph of course, but at least Kenny hasn't been teasing her quite so much as she did before.

We're nearly at the playground now. Can you see it, just at the corner of the street?

Everyone's there by the look of it. Fliss seems to be recreating her exploits on the assault course for about the hundredth time. And Kenny looks as though she's about to swing for her. Come on, we'd better hurry up and join Frankie and Rosie in trying to keep the peace. It doesn't look as though our reputation for good sportsmanship is going to last that long, does it?!

Anastasia Krupnik

Anastasia opened her green notebook and, in a secret corner, very small, she wrote the most terrible name she could think of. She closed the notebook, and smiled.

Anastasia Krupnik is ten, and two very important things are happening to her: A small pink wart appears on her left thumb: and she discovers that she'll soon be having a quite unnecessary baby brother.

Serious action is called for, but the only reason she hasn't left home yet is that she has been allowed to choose the baby's name...

Order Form

To order direct from the publishers, just make a list of the titles you want and fill in the form below:

Name ....

Address ....

....

....

Send to: Dept 6, HarperCollins Publishers Ltd, Westerhill Road, Bishopbriggs, Glasgow G64 2QT.

Please enclose a cheque or postal order to the value of the cover price, plus:

UK & BFPO: Add £1.00 for the first book, and 25p per copy for each additional book ordered.

Overseas and Eire: Add £2.95 service charge. Books will be sent by surface mail but quotes for airmail despatch will be given on request.

A 24-hour telephone ordering service is available to holders of Visa, MasterCard, Amex or Switch cards on 0141- 772 2281.

Collins
An *Imprint* of HarperCollins*Publishers*